LEGO® EXO·FORCE™

COLLECTOR'S GUIDE

BY ALLISON LASSIEUR

SCHOLASTIC INC.

New York   Toronto   London   Auckland   Sydney

Mexico City   New Delhi   Hong Kong   Buenos Aires

ISBN-13: 978-0-439-82811-6
ISBN-10: 0-439-82811-2

12 11 10 9 8 7 6 5 4 3 2 1   7 8 9 10 11/0
Printed in the U.S.A.

First printing, March 2007

TABLE OF CONTENTS

EXPLOSIVE

CONGRATULATIONS

If you are reading this, you have been chosen to train as an EXO-FORCE pilot. This job requires strength, courage, and teamwork. Training will not be easy. Only the best will make it through to become an elite member of the EXO-FORCE team.

You will be stationed on Sentai Mountain, which is split into two halves. We humans live on the northern peak and the robots control the southern peak. The two halves of the mountain are joined by many bridges. These bridges have been the site of several critical battles between the humans and robots. It is up to you, the EXO-FORCE pilots, to guard the human side of Sentai Mountain against our robot enemy.

All of the information in this training manual is of great importance and highly classified. It will explain the history of Sentai Mountain and the rise of the robot enemy. It will describe the battle machines you will be using and those of your robot enemies. If you make it through the training, you will possess the knowledge and skills of a true EXO-FORCE pilot. Study this manual thoroughly. Remember: Your life may depend on it.

Long ago, humans lived on both sides of the mountain. The northern slope was filled with farming villages. We built factories deep within mountain caves. Mining was carried out on the southern slope, using special mining robots. The robots were designed to lift heavy objects and go into areas that were too dangerous for humans.

Then something went terribly wrong. The robots malfunctioned and turned their mining armor into battle machines. The robots attacked the humans, their violence spreading from robot to robot, as if it were a contagious virus.

陸軍

SENTAI MOUNTAIN

Even today, our scientists still do not know why the robots turned on us. We were taken completely by surprise by their attack, but we were in greater peril than we knew. The robots had unleashed powerful forces deep within Sentai Mountain. This violent power grew as robots and humans fought one another. Finally, it split Sentai Mountain in two.

While unprepared for battle, we did what we could to fight back. Although many human lives were lost, we were able to drive the robots and their battle machines into the gorge between the mountain peaks and seal them beneath tons of rocks. The robots were defeated.

After the robot rebellion, the spirits of the humans were badly broken. Everyone lost a friend or loved one in the horrible attack. And now our beloved Sentai Mountain was broken as well.

Slowly our people began the long process of rebuilding our homes and villages. We also needed to create bridges that would span the two peaks and connect the villages and people of Sentai Mountain.

Our engineers built many different kinds of bridges. Some are simple structures made of wood used by locals to travel from one peak to the other. Others are made out of metal with strong gates. These were built to withstand even the most powerful earthquake. The largest and strongest of these bridges is Tenchi Bridge.

Once the rebuilding and bridges were complete, and the terrible robot battle was behind us, life began to return to normal.

OR SO WE THOUGHT.

CREATION OF THE
EXO-FORCE TEAM

While things were peaceful for a time, many feared that the robots would return. As a result, the humans built a group of battle machines that were designed to defend Sentai Mountain and fight against the robots, should they ever return.

Our battle machines utilized the latest technology and weaponry and required a specially trained force to pilot them in battle. We recruited the best and the brightest to learn how to use the battle machines. They trained to fight the robots and studied how to work together to defeat the enemy. We called this elite team the EXO-FORCE.

The EXO-FORCE team included many young pilots just like you who showed extraordinary skills and courage. These pilots knew that our survival was in their hands. Now, you are our next hope in defeating the enemy.

SECOND ROBOT
REBELLION

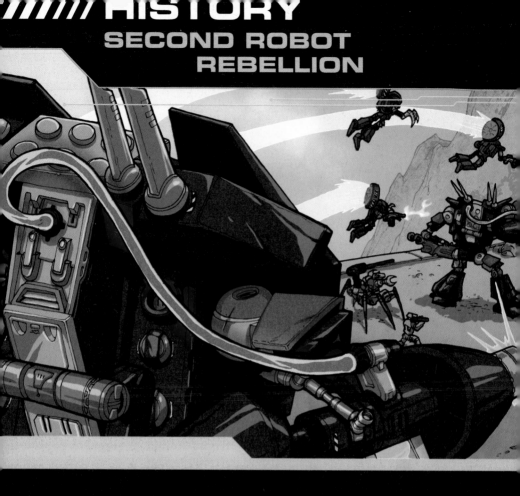

Just as many had believed, the robots were not defeated when humans cast them into the gorge. While in the gorge, the robots had become more powerful than we imagined. They repaired themselves and rebuilt their battle machines. They rose from the gorge and attacked us once again.

This time we were ready. The newly formed EXO-FORCE team charged into battle. When the robots tried to cross the bridges, EXO-FORCE pilots drove them back. Again and again the robots attacked. Each time, the EXO-FORCE team stopped them. The battle raged for days, and hundreds of robots were destroyed. Finally the robot army retreated and the second robot rebellion came to an end.

We had won, but at great cost. Many EXO-FORCE pilots did not survive. The robots captured pilots and other humans, and our battle machines were either badly damaged or destroyed. Slowly, we rebuilt the battle machines and recruited new pilots for EXO-FORCE. Now we are as strong as ever.

BUT SO IS THE ROBOT ARMY.

We do not know when the robots will attack next. But they will attack again. The robots will never stop until humans are destroyed. The EXO-FORCE team is the only thing that stands between us and our destruction by the robot enemy.

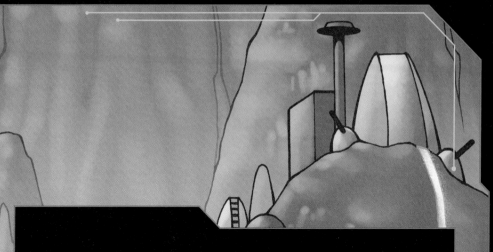

The primary reason for the creation of the EXO-FORCE team is to guard the bridges against robot attack. All of the training that you will go through has this single purpose in mind. You and your fellow pilots are our first and best defense against the robot forces.

Make no mistake: The robots are masters at upgrading their battle machines with the latest powerful technology. To survive, we humans must not only keep up—we must surpass the robots' technology. Our very existence depends on our ability to build new machines and train EXO-FORCE pilots to run them.

The EXO-FORCE team's greatest strengths are creativity, courage, and teamwork—concepts the robots will never understand.

An EXO-FORCE pilot must be willing to fight to the death, no matter what the odds. The entire human race depends on the skills of the EXO-FORCE for their very survival.

YOU CANNOT WAVER.

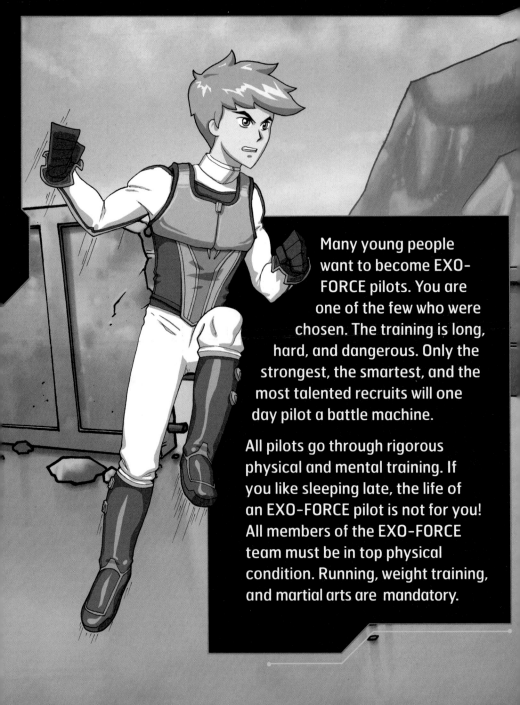

Many young people want to become EXO-FORCE pilots. You are one of the few who were chosen. The training is long, hard, and dangerous. Only the strongest, the smartest, and the most talented recruits will one day pilot a battle machine.

All pilots go through rigorous physical and mental training. If you like sleeping late, the life of an EXO-FORCE pilot is not for you! All members of the EXO-FORCE team must be in top physical condition. Running, weight training, and martial arts are mandatory.

While each new pilot will be assigned a specific battle machine, each EXO-FORCE pilot must know how to operate every type of battle machine. You will memorize every wire, every bolt, and every circuit in each battle machine. All EXO-FORCE recruits will spend time in the computer center studying math, science, engineering, and computer programming.

Every recruit will be trained in the latest computer and weapons technology. You will spend a great deal of time in the battle-machine simulator, fighting mock battles with fellow recruits. On the weapons range you will practice using laser rifles, laser cannons, missile launchers, and laser guns. There will be no weapon or machine that each one of you cannot use effectively in battle.

HIKARU

RYO

These elite **EXO-FORCE** pilots are the best of the best. They have defended us against many robot attacks.

TAKESHI

HA-YA-TO

These pilots have the courage and skill that all EXO-FORCE pilots should work to achieve.

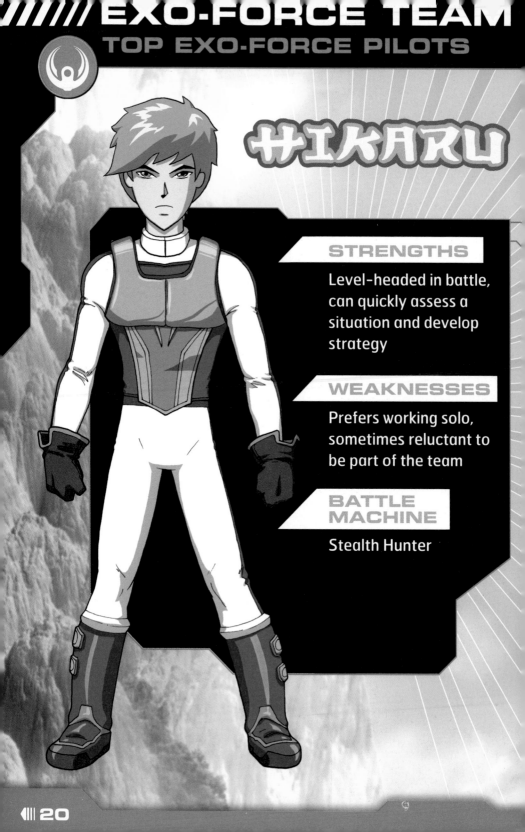

HIKARU

STRENGTHS

Level-headed in battle, can quickly assess a situation and develop strategy

WEAKNESSES

Prefers working solo, sometimes reluctant to be part of the team

BATTLE MACHINE

Stealth Hunter

龍翼

BACKGROUND

Hikaru worked on a robot ranch before the first rebellion. It was his job to ride and test transport machines, then fine-tune them. It was risky work, but Hikaru did it with coolness and strength. He became an expert in handling robots and their capabilities— excellent skills for an EXO-FORCE pilot to have.

After the first robot rebellion Hikaru volunteered for the newly formed EXO-FORCE team. He was assigned the Stealth Hunter and soon became an expert. He was one of the few EXO-FORCE pilots to survive the second rebellion.

Do not underestimate Hikaru. He may not talk much, but he knows what he is doing. He is independent, but he can be counted on in a fight.

RYO

STRENGTHS

Never sits still, extremely resourceful, can fix machinery or weaponry with little effort

WEAKNESSES

Is sometimes too busy doing everything at once to focus on details

BATTLE MACHINE

Uplink

龍翼

BACKGROUND

If anything needs fixing, Ryo is the one to do it. Before the first rebellion, Ryo was a master repair tech for a large factory on the northern slope. There is no circuit, no gear, no weapon that Ryo cannot fix. After the robots rebelled, Ryo joined the design team that developed the Grand Titan battle machine.

Ryo asked to become an EXO-FORCE pilot, but was refused. His skills in maintenance and development were more valuable on the ground. In his typical hot-headed manner, he designed his own, special battle machine, Uplink. As you will see, the Uplink battle machine has tremendous fire power and maneuverability.

We discovered that Ryo's skills as a pilot are excellent. He convinced us that his place was in the middle of battle, and we agreed. His quick thinking has saved EXO-FORCE in battle many times. Oh, and don't try to keep up with Ryo. It is impossible.

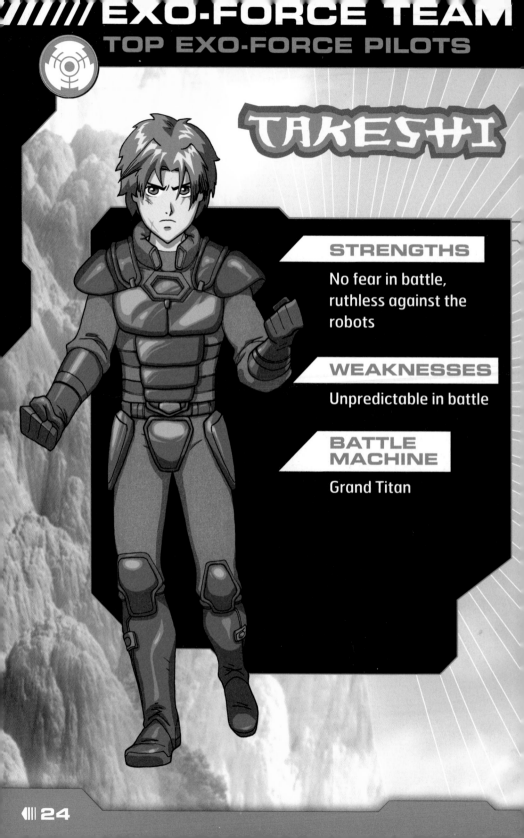

TAKESHI

STRENGTHS

No fear in battle, ruthless against the robots

WEAKNESSES

Unpredictable in battle

BATTLE MACHINE

Grand Titan

龍
翼

BACKGROUND

Before the rebellion, Takeshi was a miner on the southern peak. He worked alongside some of the very robots that are now our enemy. During the second rebellion he was separated from his family, as were many of us. Recently, however, his family was located and rescued from the robots.

Takeshi takes a lot of chances in battle—sometimes too many—and has defeated more robots than any other EXO-FORCE pilot. He has trouble working as a team with the other EXO-FORCE pilots. He rarely rests. Any recruit who wants to find Takeshi will usually find him in his battle machine or in the training complex. He was surprised by the robots once. He does not intend to let it happen again.

HA-YA-TO

STRENGTHS

A fearless pilot, willing to try any maneuver or plan that will defeat the robots

WEAKNESSES

Takes unnecessary risks, doesn't always take the robot threat seriously

BATTLE MACHINE

Gate Defender

ナ-ヤ-ナ口

龍
翼

BACKGROUND

Ha-Ya-To joined the force after the second robot rebellion. His specialty is flying, and he can always be found in the air or in his battle machine, the Gate Defender. He has loved to fly since he was a child. But he rarely talks about his early life, as his entire family (along with their industrial village) was destroyed in the second robot rebellion.

Ha-Ya-To generally serves as a back-line pilot, ready to jump into combat when needed. He is a master of gate defense, using Gate Defender to destroy invading robot armies. His flying skills have been invaluable to EXO-FORCE. He has saved many battles with his quick thinking and keen eye. He meets all threats with a laugh and a loop-and-roll.

SENSEI KEIKEN

Keiken is the general-leader in charge of all EXO-FORCE pilots. Do not mistake his kind demeanor for weakness. He will put you in your place if you do not focus on your EXO-FORCE training.

龍
翼

Keiken is a master robotics engineer. Before the rebellion, he was one of the lead designers of the mining robots. He is convinced that if he discovers the flaw in their program he can repair it and end the robot rebellion. Some think that he is getting close to discovering the flaw that caused the robots to malfunction.

As an EXO-FORCE recruit, you will obey Sensei Keiken throughout training. He will tell you when to eat. He will tell you when to sleep. And he will teach you how to defeat the robot army. Listen to everything he says. Your lives, and the lives of all humans, may one day depend on it.

Our greatest strength against the robots are our battle machines. By the end of your training you will know all of these battle machines in great detail.

GRAND TITAN

SKY GUARDIAN

SILENT STRIKE

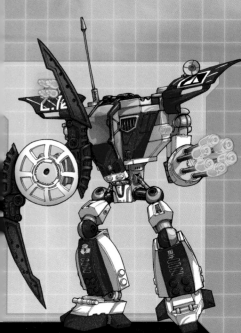

BLADE TITAN

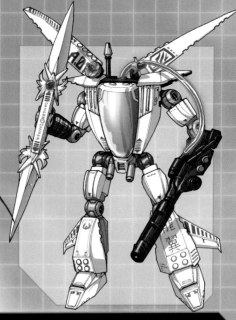

STEALTH HUNTER

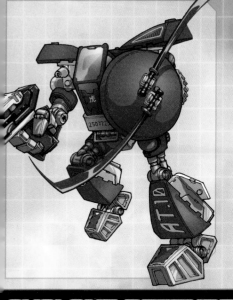

CYCLONE DEFENDER

EXO-FORCE TEAM
BATTLE MACHINES

STEALTH HUNTER

Designed for high-level spying and air strikes, the controls are tight and quick for maximum maneuvering.

PROS

Fast, light, maneuverable.

CONS

Stealth-mode reduces weapons effectiveness to 48% and speed to 56%

REQUIRED KNOWLEDGE

Extra training in computer technology, martial arts (for the electro-sword), and weapons technology

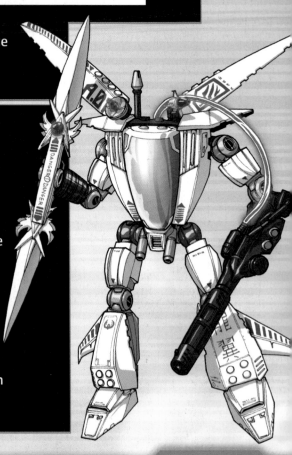

• Laser rifle is 98% accurate at full speed.

• Enhanced sensors include radar, sonar, thermo, infrared, motion, and telescopic.

• Prototype stealth coating 100% effective in stealth mode

• Magnetized nuclear plasma power source

• Intractium armor, enhanced for stealth coating

• Dual blade electro-sword with titanium/thermodium blades. Blades can cut through up to 2 feet of robot armor.

GRAND TITAN

The most powerful battle machine in the fleet.

PROS

Almost indestructible. Can inflict high rates of damage with little energy drain. Electromagnetic pulse pincers highly effective.

CONS

Sacrifices speed and maneuverability for strength and power. Vulnerable to air attack. Exposed power supply is target in battle.

REQUIRED KNOWLEDGE

Weapons technology, electromagnetic technology, military history and technique

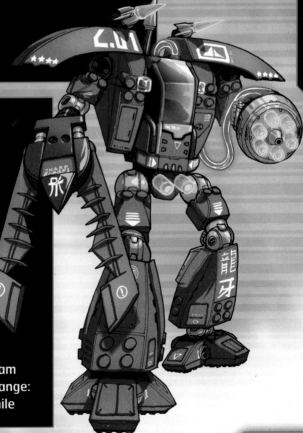

- Standard sensors, including night vision and motion sensors
- Intractium armor, enhanced 8-inch coating with electromagnetic repulsion system upgrade
- EMP pulse pincers with enhanced electromagnetic upgrades
- Magnetized nuclear plasma power source
- Laser cannon with variable beam and enhanced power supply. Range: Accurate to 97% to one-half mile

SILENT STRIKE

The only flying battle machine in the EXO-FORCE, used for recon and aerial attacks.

PROS

Highly maneuverable in battle. All weaponry enhanced for high-speed accuracy.

CONS

Lightweight armor makes this battle machine especially vulnerable to attack.

REQUIRED KNOWLEDGE

Training in aerodynamics, sensors, flight training, and weapons systems

- Goes from 0-200 mph in 20 seconds

- Enhanced sensors, including night vision, telescopic, infrared, thermo, and motion sensors

- Laser cannons with enhanced altitude adjustment upgrades. Range: 95% accurate to altitudes of up to one mile

- Magnetized nuclear plasma power source

BLADE TITAN

Recently discovered in , this machine will become the front-line defense in the EXO-FORCE arsenal.

PROS

Heavy armor and weapons make this battle machine a powerhouse in battle.

CONS

Extreme weight makes this battle machine slow and vulnerable to attack.

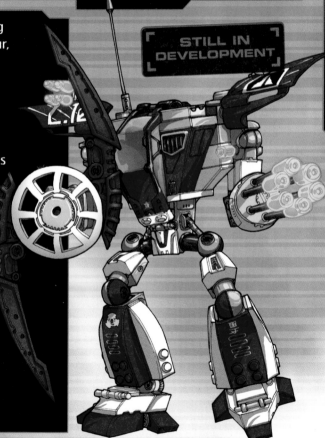

STILL IN DEVELOPMENT

- Enhanced sensors, including motion, infrared, radar, sonar, and telescopic
- Intractium armor, 4-inch base coating, with 4-inch enhanced coating of unknown material
- Dual proton cannon, delivers a laser-enhanced blast of energy 98% accurate to 600 yards
- Enhanced shield technology with reflective capabilities. Can deflect enemy fire and redirect its full force, causing maximum damage
- Nuclear plasma power source, enhanced with unknown systems

Our engineers are still studying it to determine all its capabilities.

SKY GUARDIAN

Recently discovered in [CONFIDENTIAL], this flying machine can be used for recon and quick-strike attacks.

PROS

Lightning speed and maneuverability

CONS

High speeds burn too much energy, so weapons cannot be fired during flight.

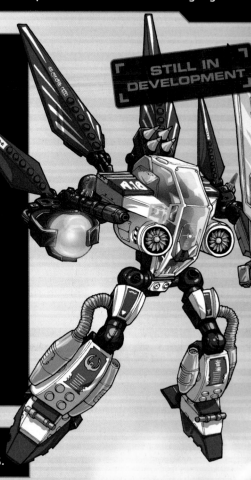

STILL IN DEVELOPMENT

- Greater speed and control than the Silent Strike, but lesser weapons capabilities

- Standard sensors, including night vision, radar, enhanced terrasensors, and motion sensors

- Intractium armor, 2-inch coating with aerodynamic enhancements

- Particle beam rifle, shoots multiple blasts of high energy in rounds of 20 per shot

- Magnetized nuclear plasma power source

- Enhance shields with superior reflective capabilities

Our engineers are still studying it to determine all its capabilities.

CYCLONE DEFENDER

Recently discovered in ⌈CONFIDENTIAL⌉, this is a powerful front-line battle machine.

PROS

Unknown at this time, although it appears to have enhanced maneuverability and shield technology.

CONS

Unknown at this time.

- Appears to have greater fire power than either Stealth Hunter or Blade Titan
- Enhanced sensors, including night vision, radar, and motion sensors. Unusual circuit boards suggest new sensor technology.
- Intractium armor, 4-inch coating reinforced with unknown material that seems to reflect enemy sensors
- Laser blasters and proton cannons with enhanced energy packs to reduce energy drains during battle
- Magnetized nuclear plasma power source

⌈STILL IN DEVELOPMENT⌋

Our engineers are still studying it to determine all its capabilities.

EXO-FORCE TEAM
BATTLE WEAPONS

All EXO-FORCE recruits will be trained to use the following standard weapons systems. Basic weapons training is mandatory for all recruits. High-level weapons training will begin after you are assigned a specific battle machine.

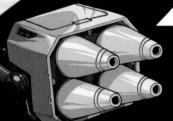

MISSILE LAUNCHER

Damage factor: High. Effective in both short- and long-range combat. Can destroy several Iron Drone robots or severely cripple a robot battle machine.

Facts to Know: Launchers require substantial energy output in short bursts. This pulls energy from other systems for brief moments, which make you temporarily vulnerable to attack. Launchers set to maximum damage can drain engines and communications. EXO-FORCE pilots using missile launchers MUST monitor all systems and energy levels during battle.

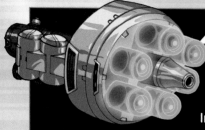

LASER CANNON

Damage Factor: High. Most effective for long-range combat. Precise aiming capabilities. One shot can destroy several Iron Drones or severely damage enemy battle machines.

Facts to Know: Laser cannons are less powerful but more precise than missile launchers. This allows EXO-FORCE pilots using them to hit specific targets for maximum damage in battle. Battle machines equipped with laser cannons have enhanced targeting systems. Cannons fire high-voltage energy balls, which are ineffective against some enemy shields.

LASER RIFLE

Damage factor: Medium to High.
Designed for short-range and speed combat. Enhanced targeting systems on all battle machines equipped with laser rifles. Highly accurate.

Facts to know: Laser rifles are high-precision weapons that do maximum damage at ranges between 10 to 100 feet. They cause no energy drain and are excellent back-up weapons in the event of a weapons drain during battle. Equipped with enhanced motion and energy sensors to pinpoint and destroy specific robot components.

LASER GUN

Damage factor: Medium to High.
Less precise than laser rifles, but more effective in very close range combat. Although they do not have the firepower to destroy the enemy, laser guns can damage and cripple attacking forces.

Facts to Know: Rotating laser guns require manual targeting capabilities for maximum effectiveness. Minimal energy drain on battle machine systems. Can fire a round of 50 laser bullet blasts per second. Good for short-range defense.

Your purpose as a member of the EXO-FORCE team is to defend humans from attack. To defend our world, you must first understand it.

FARMS

Farms once covered the northern slope of Sentai Mountain. Now only about 40% of the land is safe for farming. All of our food comes from these farming villages. It is vital that they are protected from all attacks. Each EXO-FORCE pilot will be assigned guard duty in these villages on a rotating schedule.

INDUSTRIAL VILLAGES

More than 90% of our industrial villages were destroyed in the robot rebellions. The few that were located on the northern slopes survived. Factories in these villages manufacture the equipment and components for the battle machines. Each village is heavily guarded with EXO-FORCE pilots and battle machines.

MINES

Few mines survived the robot rebellions. The surviving mines continue to produce the raw materials and metals for the factories. Their locations are highly classified and heavily guarded. Only EXO-FORCE pilots with superior security clearances are allowed to guard the mines.

HANGAR

Location where all battle machines are docked for refueling and repair. At the northern end of the hangar is the battle simulation arena where all EXO-FORCE recruits participate in mock battles.

TRAINING GROUND

All recruits are required to attend martial arts and physical enhancement classes on the training grounds. The southern portion of the grounds is reserved for weapons training.

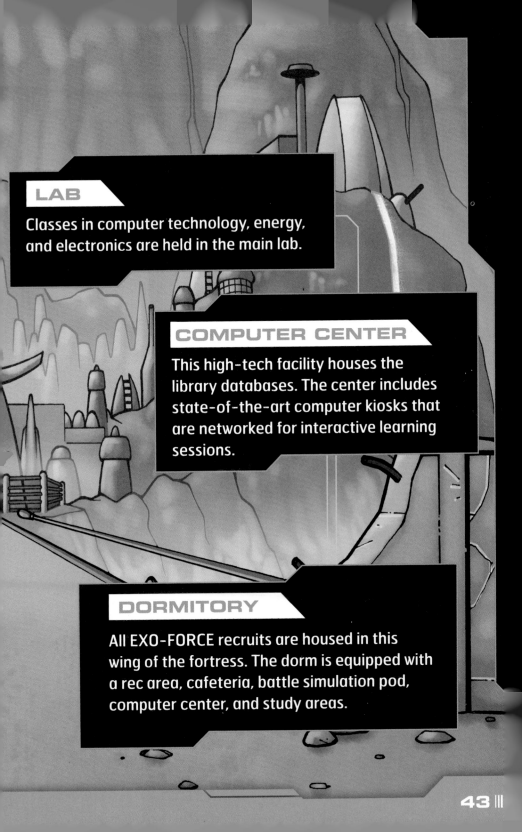

LAB

Classes in computer technology, energy, and electronics are held in the main lab.

COMPUTER CENTER

This high-tech facility houses the library databases. The center includes state-of-the-art computer kiosks that are networked for interactive learning sessions.

DORMITORY

All EXO-FORCE recruits are housed in this wing of the fortress. The dorm is equipped with a rec area, cafeteria, battle simulation pod, computer center, and study areas.

CONFIDENTIAL

CITY OF GOLD

There is a legend of a strange golden city high on Sentai Mountain. It is said that the city holds the key to defeating the robots forever. Many dismiss these stories as myths to keep our hope alive. But some, including Sensei Keiken, think there may be some truth to the stories.

He recently sent a squad of top EXO-FORCE pilots on a mission to find the mysterious City of Gold. No one believed these pilots would return from such a dangerous mission. But they did return. And they brought three new battle machines back with them. No one is sure how these machines work. But it is clear that they are very different from the machines we have now.

DID THE EXO-FORCE TEAM FIND THE MYTHICAL CITY OF GOLD?

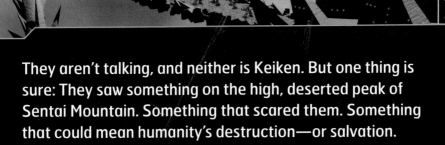

They aren't talking, and neither is Keiken. But one thing is sure: They saw something on the high, deserted peak of Sentai Mountain. Something that scared them. Something that could mean humanity's destruction—or salvation.

To defeat the enemy you must know it. Your EXO-FORCE training includes in-depth study of the robots, their components, and their methods. All known information about the robot enemy will be drilled into your head until you think you are a robot. Then you will be ready to fight them.

STRENGTHS

Relentless and ruthless. Robots are unable to feel pain, anger, or fatigue. They have the ability to self-repair. They will sacrifice huge numbers of themselves and their battle machines to achieve their objective.

WEAKNESSES

Robots cannot think independently of their programming, which makes them vulnerable to surprise moves. Their belief in their superiority makes them underestimate us. They are slow to change programming or tactics during battle.

MECA ONE

This was the first robot to rebel against the humans. It is the cold, ruthless leader of the robots. After the first rebellion defeat, Meca One created several clones of itself. If Meca One is destroyed, a clone will immediately take its place. Destroying Meca One is useless.

HOW TO DEFEAT IT

Meca One is the only robot, we believe, that has been programmed to exhibit emotion. Its actions suggest that it feels ambition to rule, as well as anger and hatred toward humans. Keiken theorizes that the key to defeating Meca One is to use its emotion programming against it.

DRONES

WHAT WE KNOW

Drones are the pawns of the robot army. They are produced by the thousands and will swarm onto a battlefield in huge numbers in Sentry battle machines. They are manufactured with high-quality armor that is difficult to penetrate with most standard EXO-FORCE weapons.

HOW TO DEFEAT THEM

A combination of long-range missile launchers and short-range laser rifles are most effective against large Drone attacks. WARNING: Any Drones that survive a first attack will self-repair and shield their vulnerable areas. Immediate, critical hits are vital to success.

DEVASTATORS

Devastators are almost as strong as Drones, but they have greater agility. They have the ability to adapt to changes in battle and to develop new programming. It is believed that each Devastator is networked directly to Meca One, who controls their actions.

HOW TO DEFEAT THEM

Out think them. Devastators are particularly vulnerable to unusual or unexpected battle strategies. They are also incapable of understanding strategies that rely on teamwork for success. EXO-FORCE pilots who devise teamwork-oriented battle plans are guaranteed victory.

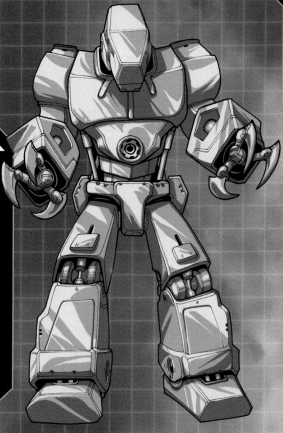

THUNDER FURY

These battle machines are piloted by Devastator robots. Expect them to develop strategy during battle. Don't even think about trying to destroy a Thunder Fury. It is almost impossible. However, it can be disabled.

STRENGTHS

High-quality, 8-inch tenatium resistant to almost all EXO-FORCE weaponry. Only the Grand Titan laser cannons are effective against this armor.

Agile and easily maneuverable in all kinds of terrain. Fast.

WEAKNESSES

These battle machines burn through their magnetized nuclear plasma power supplies very quickly. EXO-FORCE strategies that require them to use power will disable them.

COMPONENTS

- Standard sensors with night vision, telescopic, infrared
- Enhanced communications with auto scramble upgrade, 5-mile range
- Titanium power saw is especially effective against our armor. The best defense against this weapon: Don't get too close.
- Auto laser cannon: similar to our laser cannon with enhanced targeting upgrades

FIRE VULTURE

These air battle machines are piloted by Devastators. These fierce machines made the initial strikes against humans in the rebellion. The robots usually include several Fire Vultures in any frontal assault.

STRENGTHS

Fast and agile in the air.

Magnetized nuclear plasma power supplies include energy upgrade, allowing them to stay in battle for longer periods.

Effective long-range weaponry.

WEAKNESSES

Thinner armor means that the Fire Vultures can be destroyed with most standard EXO-FORCE weapons.

Heavy weapons are powerful but sluggish. A direct hit will cripple targeting systems.

COMPONENTS

- Enhanced sensors including night vision, telescope zoom, infrared, 360-degree vision, upgraded mobile targeting array
- Enhanced communications with auto scramble, 20-mile range
- Flamethrower includes dual boot jets and gyro-stabilizers for altitude control

SENTRY

These are the machines you will face most often in combat. They are mass-produced by the robots and are considered expendable. Designed for frontal attacks.

STRENGTHS

Sheer numbers. During battle you will face dozens, if not hundreds, of Sentries.

They do not self-repair, but there are so many that it doesn't matter.

Their heavy weapons are designed for a large-scale frontal attack.

WEAKNESSES

Sentries are not designed to hold up in battle. Grand Titans and Stealth Hunters are especially effective against large armies of Sentries.

Shoulder and joint armor is weak. Laser gun and laser rifle shots to these points can immobilize or destroy a Sentry.

COMPONENTS

- Standard sensors with night vision and motion sensors
- Enhanced communications with auto scramble, 5-mile range
- Heavy rocket launcher is an excellent short-range weapon—energy rockets can destroy a Stealth Hunter.
- Tenatium armor, 6 inches
- Magnetized nuclear plasma power source

STRIKING VENOM

One of the newest robot battle machines, it is big, it is ugly, and it is hard to destroy. It was only the quick thinking of the senior EXO-FORCE team that defeated this battle machine.

STRENGTHS

Its insect-like body design makes it highly stable on rocky terrain.

Special leg claws can grasp any object, enhanced with crush-control upgrades.

WEAKNESSES

More legs mean more ways to bring them down.

Underside of cockpit especially vulnerable to a close-range attack

COMPONENTS

- Enhanced sensors with motion, telescopic zoom, infrared, radar
- Enhanced communications with auto scramble, 10-mile radius
- Heavy laser cannons mounted on top are highly shielded, 360ffi range
- Tenatium armor, 12 inches
- Magnetized nuclear plasma power source

SONIC PHANTOM

This air machine is the first robot-designed battle machine. It is one of the robot's most dangerous and effective weapons. Fortunately, there are only a few Sonic Phantoms in existence; we estimate no more than six.

STRENGTHS

Impenetrable armor makes the Sonic Phantom almost indestructible.

Air speeds of up to 2,700 mph, making it almost impossible to land a direct hit.

WEAKNESSES

Almost no sensors. A talented (some might say crazy) EXO-FORCE pilot could close in enough for a surprise attack.

Limited communications ability means that the Sonic Phantom cannot report on current battle conditions.

Nuclear engines are vulnerable by a direct hit from a missile launcher.

COMPONENTS

- 35-foot wingspan
- Enhanced armor (49% tenatium, 22% titanium, 15% thermoplastic, 14% composite)
- Wide-angle laser cannon effective against most EXO-FORCE battle machines
- Rotating laser guns have an airspeed accuracy of 94%

IRON CONDOR

The Iron Condor is one of the robot's newest battle machines. It is unknown when it was developed, or how many there are. Little is currently known about the Iron Condor. However, we expect that we will see more of this battle machine in the future.

STRENGTHS

Its metal wings give it enhanced flying capabilities.

Agile and fast in the air

Magnetic enhanced rockets with targeting upgrades

WEAKNESSES

It appears that the Iron Condor's lightweight armor may make it vulnerable to attack.

Direct hits to wings will disable aerial programming.

COMPONENTS

- Aerial-enhanced armor (60% thermoplastic, 20% composite, 12% tenatium, 8% titanium)
- Enhance laser cannon with aerial and targeting upgrades
- Standard communications with aerial booster, 10-mile range
- Enhanced sensors with telescopic zoom, terrasensors, motion

SHADOW CRAWLERS

This robot battle machine has been seen only once, so very little is known about it. It appears that the robots developed the Shadow Crawler as a psychological weapon.

STRENGTHS

Each Shadow Crawler is equipped with a clear pod mounted on top that contains a human prisoner.

Cloaking device with enhanced scanner scramble hides these battle machines from standard EXO-FORCE sensors

WEAKNESSES

Unknown

COMPONENTS

- Enhanced rocket launcher and laser cannon with silencer upgrades
- Multiple legs with enhanced silent-movement shock absorbers
- Composite armor with sensor shielding properties

CLAW CRUSHER

The newest battle machine designed for use by Iron Drones, the Claw Crusher is mass-produced much like the Sentry. Also like the Sentry, it is considered expendable by the robots — therefore armor is sacrificed in favor of better armament. Claw Crushers are designed to attack en masse — so where one by itself might not seem overly formidable, dozens or hundreds working together are almost unbeatable.

SPECIFICATIONS

Land-based robot battle machine

Armor: Eight inches tenatium armor

Weapons: Rotating blaster cannons; powerful ripping claws

Power Source: Magnetized nuclear plasma

Pilot: 1

All EXO-FORCE recruits will be trained in robot weapons technology. You must learn how their weapons work to defeat them in battle. When possible, you will be able to use actual robot weapons. Others will be reproductions or rebuilds of how we believe the weapons look, shoot, and handle.

LASER CANNON

Damage factor: High. The energy balls are enhanced with electromagnetic static that can fry most electronic and computer systems.

Facts to Know: This robot-enhanced weapon is less accurate than standard laser cannons. Agile EXO-FORCE pilots can usually dodge this weapon.

TITANIUM POWER SAW

Damage factor: Extremely High. This is not a weapon to mess with. If a Thunder Fury points this at you in battle, get away. If you don't, it will slice through your battle machine in an instant. We'll be picking up the pieces for weeks . . . if we survive.

Facts to Know: This technology was originally created for heavy mining equipment to drill through titanium deposits. This nasty weapon can easily cut through most EXO-FORCE battle machine armor.

ELECTRO VULTURE CLAW

Damage factor: High. Equipped on all Fire Vultures, this weapon can tear chunks out of an EXO-FORCE battle machine armor. Don't get too close to this one, either.

Facts to Know: This weapon is effective only at very close range. Fully extended, it can reach 50 feet. A clean shot at a fully extended claw can usually cut it off.

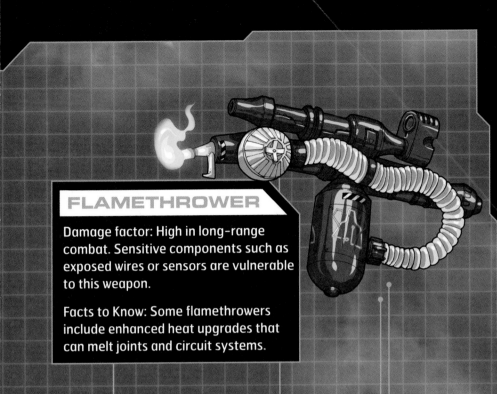

FLAMETHROWER

Damage factor: High in long-range combat. Sensitive components such as exposed wires or sensors are vulnerable to this weapon.

Facts to Know: Some flamethrowers include enhanced heat upgrades that can melt joints and circuit systems.

ROCKET LAUNCHER

Damage factor: High to Medium. Usually shot from multiple Sentries at once, which makes it extremely dangerous—and effective.

Facts to Know: Standard weapon for all Sentry battle machines. Decreased accuracy at ranges greater than 200 feet.

The robot base is located on the southern peak of Sentai Mountain. It consists of a large, blackened complex heavily guarded by robot battle machines.

Very little is known about the robot base. Recon missions have only brought back sketchy information. Future missions to the base will, hopefully, give us facts we can use to destroy it. The following is what we have learned so far.

COMMAND CENTER

We believe that a single main command center is located somewhere near the center of the base. This is where Meca One develops battle plans and sends out orders. This is also the location of the computer network that controls all robots.

ASSEMBLY LINE

We suspect that there are several robot assembly lines located throughout the complex. Some build Drones and Sentries while others reconstruct and enhance weapons systems for the battle machines.

STORAGE FACILITY

Robots that are not yet online are housed in vast storage warehouses in several locations. At activation, they are plugged into the main systems and standard battle programs are installed.

BATTLE PROGRAM DOWLOAD COMPLEX

Existing robots are brought here for systems repairs and upgrades. All new battle plans from Meca One are routed to this complex, where they are downloaded into every robot prior to an attack.

PRISONS

We believe that the Robot Base includes an underground prison where human hostages are held. We do not know how many humans may be imprisoned there. We fear it could be hundreds, perhaps thousands.

This manual is only the beginning of your training to become a top EXO-FORCE pilot. From here, you must keep studying all ways of the EXO-FORCE. If you are one of the few who completes the training, you will truly be the best of the best. You will also be part of something bigger: As an elite EXO-FORCE pilot, you are the first line of defense against the robots. Our enemy is strong. They are determined to eliminate all humans. It is up to us to prevent it.

We have fought many battles against the robot enemy. There will certainly be many more battles to come. We will keep fighting the robots until they are defeated completely. That is why you are here.

Again, congratulations and welcome to EXO-FORCE. This is not a job to be taken lightly. The survival of humankind depends on you.

GOOD LUCK.